THE ★ ★ ★ ★ ★
PRESIDENT
OF THE UNITED STATES

Written by Alice Leonhardt

STECK-VAUGHN
A Harcourt Company

www.steck-vaughn.com

CHAPTER	PAGE

Introduction 3

1   The First President 4

2   The President's Job 9

3   The White House 14

4   A Day in the Life of the President 20

5   Presidents are People 25

6   Electing the President 33

The U.S. Presidents 36

Glossary 38

Index 40

INTRODUCTION

Ever since 1789, the American people have elected a President every four years. It's hard to go through a day without seeing the President on TV or reading about the President in the newspapers.

The President has a great deal of power. He talks to kings and queens and famous people. His job seems exciting and important, and it is. The President's job is to serve the American people, to protect them, and to lead them.

President Bill Clinton at work

CHAPTER 1
THE FIRST PRESIDENT

The United States of America hasn't always had a President or even states. The country didn't even start out as one **nation**. It started out as 13 **colonies** that belonged to Great Britain. Some of Great Britain's rules for the colonies made the colonists angry. They decided they wanted to be free. In 1776 the colonies declared themselves free from Great Britain. The result was the Revolutionary War, in which George Washington led the American forces.

Seven years later, the colonists won the war, and the colonies became states. In 1787 men from 12 of the states wrote a plan for a new **government**. George Washington led these men as they turned 13 separate states into one nation that could govern itself. The plan was called the United States Constitution.

The Constitution created a **federal** system of government. In a federal system, power is divided between a national government (also called the federal government) and the governments of the states.

General George Washington during the Revolutionary War

The writers of the Constitution knew that governments often took on as much power as they could. To keep the federal government of the United States from becoming too powerful, they divided it into three branches, or parts. One of these branches is called the **Executive Branch**. It has the power to carry out and enforce laws. The writers of the Constitution decided that the head of the Executive Branch would lead the government. Some people wanted this new leader to be called "His Elective Majesty." In the end, the writers decided that the leader would be called the President of the United States.

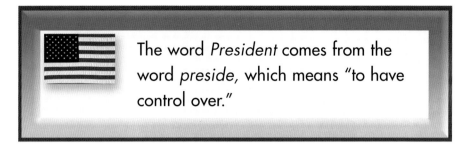

The word *President* comes from the word *preside,* which means "to have control over."

The writers of the Constitution did not want the President to be as powerful as a king, so they gave the other two branches of government the power to control the President's actions.

In 1789, after the Constitution was written, George Washington became the first President of the United States. He took the oath of office, which is a promise to "preserve, protect, and defend the Constitution of the United States." Then he began to figure out how a President should act. He knew he had an important job. At that time, he was the only leader in the world who had been **elected**. Kings and queens ruled many of the other countries. Washington did not want to rule like a king, but he wanted to act as grand as a king. He wore fine clothes and worried about manners. He sometimes traveled in a fancy carriage pulled by six white horses. But he also spent his own money to set up his office.

George Washington worried about his new job. He wanted to set a good example for other Presidents to follow. He **appointed** four people to give him advice on running the country. These advisors were called his **Cabinet**. Every President since Washington has had one. Washington's Cabinet included Alexander Hamilton, the Secretary of the Treasury. With Hamilton's help, Washington set up a national bank. He also set up a national mint to print money.

Washington stood six feet tall and was strong in mind as well as body. He owned a large farm and used his knowledge of science to become a better farmer.

Washington was not a talkative man, but when he spoke, he spoke wisely and to the point. At times he was slow to make up his mind. However, once George Washington made a decision, he always followed through with it.

President George Washington

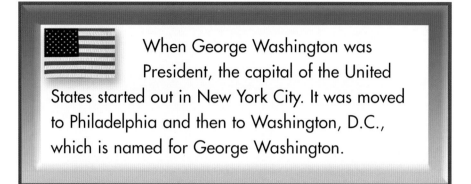
When George Washington was President, the capital of the United States started out in New York City. It was moved to Philadelphia and then to Washington, D.C., which is named for George Washington.

Washington served two four-year **terms** as President. He died on December 14, 1799. He is known as the father of his country because he helped to create the United States of America. Because of Washington's strong leadership and good judgment, he was "first in war, first in peace, and first in the hearts of his countrymen."

CHAPTER 2
THE PRESIDENT'S JOB

When the Constitution of the United States was written, the writers did not list every one of the President's duties. They depended on George Washington to work out many of the President's responsibilities. They knew he would set a good example for the Presidents to come. Today the President has many duties that keep him very, very busy.

CHIEF EXECUTIVE

Because the President is the head of the Executive Branch of the government, he is often called the Chief Executive. In this role he must make sure that all of the country's laws and **treaties** are carried out. He must decide how much money the country should spend and prepare a budget. He must also direct all the groups of people that carry out the business of the country.

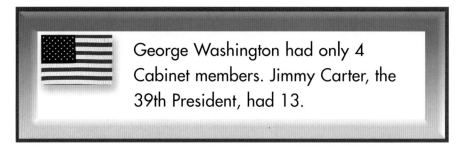

George Washington had only 4 Cabinet members. Jimmy Carter, the 39th President, had 13.

The members of the President's Cabinet are part of the Executive Branch. Cabinet members advise the President. All are heads of important departments of government, such as education, health, and energy.

As Chief Executive, the President has emergency powers. These powers allow him to end or prevent emergencies that threaten national safety or health. The President can also give executive orders. These orders are statements or directions that have the force of laws. President Lincoln gave an executive order in 1863 when he declared that all slaves were free.

COMMANDER-IN-CHIEF

The President is also the leader of the United States **military**. His job is to make sure the country is safe in times of peace and that it is protected in times of war. As Commander-in-Chief, the President is in charge of the Army, Navy, Air Force, and Marines. He can send troops overseas. However, the President cannot declare war on another country.

HEAD OF STATE

Another of the President's jobs is to represent the American government. The President goes to special celebrations such as the opening of a national park. He travels all over the United States and to many foreign countries. He invites leaders of other countries to the United States and the White House. He also gives awards to war heroes and invites important Americans to the White House.

President Ronald Reagan with his Cabinet

DIRECTOR OF FOREIGN AFFAIRS

One of the most difficult of the President's jobs is to direct the United States' relationships with **foreign** countries. The President appoints people to travel to other countries and represent the United States. The President has the power to make treaties with other countries to end wars or disagreements. He can refuse to talk with new foreign governments. He can also suggest laws that help them. Some Presidents have acted as world peacemakers. They have helped other countries to work out problems. For example, Woodrow Wilson helped work out the peace treaty that ended World War I.

LAWMAKING LEADER

The President cannot pass new laws. Only **Congress** can do that. However, one of the President's jobs is to

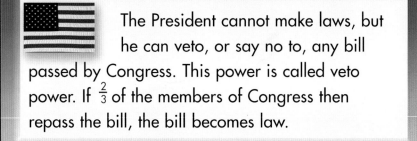

The President cannot make laws, but he can veto, or say no to, any bill passed by Congress. This power is called veto power. If $\frac{2}{3}$ of the members of Congress then repass the bill, the bill becomes law.

suggest new laws. These proposed laws are called bills. Each year, the President gives a speech to Congress called the State of the Union Address. In his speech, he describes bills that he would like Congress to turn into laws.

THE LEADER OF THE AMERICAN PEOPLE

Perhaps the most important of all the President's jobs is to serve all Americans, not just one state or one person. To lead and inform the American people, he must communicate with them. Early Presidents made speeches to groups of people. Later Presidents used radio. Franklin Roosevelt talked to Americans on radio programs he called "fireside chats." Roosevelt also used TV to speak to Americans. He was the first President to do this. Since the 1960s, Presidents have mainly used TV to communicate with the people of America.

President Franklin Roosevelt giving a fireside chat

CHAPTER 3
THE WHITE HOUSE

The President and his family live in the White House. At first it was called the President's Palace, the President's House, and the Executive Mansion. In 1798 the outside walls were painted white. People began calling it the White House. In 1902 Theodore Roosevelt made the name "White House" **official**.

The White House began when George Washington decided that the First Family needed a home. In 1792 he held a contest to find the best design. Nine people entered the contest. Washington wanted the President's home to be grand and beautiful, but he didn't want it to look like a castle. A man named James Hoban won the contest with his beautiful design.

Workers spent eight years building the White House. It had two floors, stone walls, and 30 rooms. At that time it was the biggest house in America! President Washington guided the building of the White House, but he never lived in it. The second President, John

The White House in 1807

Adams, was the first President to live in the White House. When he and his wife, Abigail, first moved in, the White House wasn't quite finished. It had no running water and little heat. Abigail had to hang the wash in the East Room.

The White House has gone through many changes over the years. During the War of 1812, the British burned it. Rebuilding took three years. As time went on, the West Wing and East Wing were added. In 1929 the West Wing burned and had to be rebuilt. In 1948 President Harry Truman realized that the White House needed major work. "I've had the second floor where we live examined," he wrote his sister, "and it is about to fall down!" Work to repair the White House began in 1949. It grew to 100 rooms. A laundry, staff kitchen, and barber shop were added.

15

The White House today

Today the White House has 132 rooms, including 35 bathrooms and 28 fireplaces. It has a tennis court, jogging track, swimming pool, movie theater, and a bowling lane. It takes about $730 million a year to run the White House and pay its staff of 91 workers. They include florists, secretaries, cooks, and housekeepers. Even though the White House has changed over the years, the stone walls that make up the outside of the house are the same ones put in place more than 200 years ago.

The First Family lives on the second floor of the White House. The rooms on these floors are private. The family decorates them with their own things. The

Secret Service agents follow the members of the First Family everywhere. They even check the President's food to make sure it's safe to eat. The agents are trained to deal with all kinds of emergencies.

President's office is in the West Wing of the White House. The Cabinet Room, where the President meets with Cabinet members, and the Vice-President's office are also in the West Wing.

The White House is the President's home and office, but many rooms are open to visitors. Visitors can tour first-floor rooms, which include the Blue Room, the East Room, and the State Dining Room. Free tickets are available at the White House Visitors Office. Lines are long, since the White House receives 6000 visitors a day!

The Blue Room

THE WHITE HOUSE

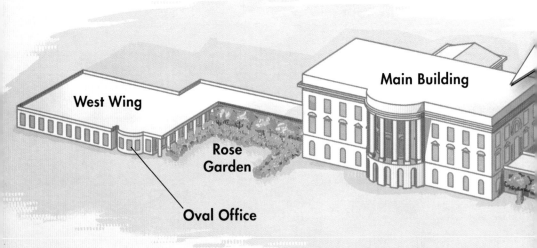

West Wing

Main Building

Rose
Garden

Oval Office

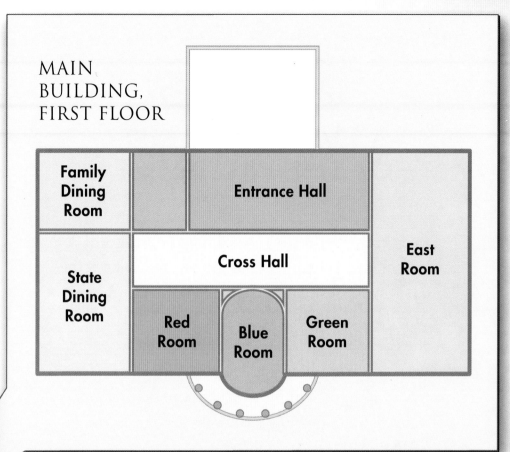

MAIN BUILDING, FIRST FLOOR

Family Dining Room

Entrance Hall

Cross Hall

State Dining Room

East Room

Red Room

Blue Room

Green Room

East Wing

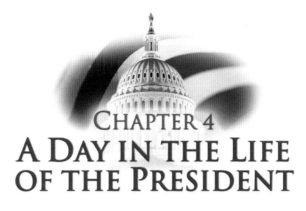

CHAPTER 4
A DAY IN THE LIFE OF THE PRESIDENT

Many early Presidents worked only in the morning. Since then, the government has grown, and so have the President's responsibilities. Today's President works all day and into the night.

The President usually begins each day by watching the news on TV and reading several newspapers. He may meet with his staff over breakfast to discuss the latest news. It's important for him to keep up with everything that goes on in the world.

After breakfast the President heads to the West Wing to meet with other members of the Executive Branch of government. They inform him on important matters. The President also meets with his secretary to find out his schedule for the day. He may attend a Cabinet meeting, where he listens to the heads of his departments. Sometimes he speaks to reporters at a **press conference**. He may meet with members of

The Oval Office of the White House

Congress to discuss new laws. Some meetings take ten minutes. Others stretch into hours.

During the day and sometimes at night, the President works in his office, which is called the Oval Office. There he answers the phone, answers e-mail messages, reads reports, and signs important papers.

As part of his day, the President may also prepare for a trip. As a world leader, the President meets with many people. As Head of State, he travels all over the United States and the world. For long trips the President and his staff use Air Force One, a jet airplane. Two of these jets are kept at Andrews Air Force Base. Only one jet is used at a time. Each jet costs about $250 million!

An Air Force One jet

Each of the huge jets can carry up to 97 people at a time. Each has 7 bathrooms, an office for the President, and a huge dining room. The jet flies at about 600 miles an hour and needs a crew of 23 to run it.

Evenings for the President are busy, too. The President and First Lady entertain many foreign leaders, including kings and queens. When these guests arrive, they are welcomed with a ceremony on the south lawn of the White House. At the ceremony, the guests walk down a red carpet with the President. The President may also attend a State Dinner for as many as 500 guests. After dinner, musicians and dancers provide entertainment.

Being President can be an exhausting job, so most Presidents try to stay healthy and fit. President George Bush jogged three miles a day. President Ronald Reagan worked out in the gym. President Gerald Ford swam in the White House pool.

Sometimes the President takes a break from his work. He can bowl, swim, play tennis, or watch a movie with his family and friends. To do these things, he doesn't even have to leave the White House!

On the weekends, the President and First Lady may travel to Camp David, in Maryland. It's only a 30-minute ride on Marine One, the President's helicopter. At Camp David the President and his family can relax and have fun. It has a swimming pool, bowling alley, tennis court, and riding stable. The President often meets with foreign leaders at Camp David. There they can discuss important matters in private.

Holidays bring extra duties for the President. The **annual** Easter Egg Roll on the White House lawn is held every year on the Monday after Easter. Ten thousand eggs are decorated for thousands of children.

The first e-mail message was sent to the White House in 1993. By 1999 President Bill Clinton received about 4000 e-mails each day. Anyone can e-mail the President at president@whitehouse.gov.

The President's job is to blow the whistle. That's the signal for the children to start rolling their eggs across the lawn.

The winter holidays at the White House are a very busy time for the President, his family, and their staff. Preparing for the holidays starts the year before! They send as many as 300,000 holiday cards, and they decorate dozens of trees. Every year, a horse-drawn carriage brings the $18\frac{1}{2}$-foot (5.6-meter) official tree to the White House. Volunteers decorate it with 2700 lights and handmade decorations from all over the United States.

President and Mrs. John F. Kennedy during the holiday season of 1961

CHAPTER 5
PRESIDENTS ARE PEOPLE

In their public life, Presidents are important world leaders with many serious jobs to do. But they are normal people, too. Here are some interesting facts about the Presidents, their families, and their pets.

THE PRESIDENTS

George Washington was a brave general and leader, but he loved his dogs. He gave them names like Sweet Lips, Madame Moose, and True Love.

James Madison was the country's smallest President, weighing only 100 pounds (45 kilograms). His wife called him "darling little husband." Trying to look older, he powdered his hair white.

The teddy bear is named for President Theodore Roosevelt. When he was on a hunting trip in 1902, Roosevelt refused to shoot a bear cub. A toymaker heard about the incident and named a stuffed bear after Roosevelt. The teddy bear soon became very popular and still is.

President Woodrow Wilson's sheep

Woodrow Wilson, who was President during part of World War I, raised a herd of sheep on the White House lawn. The money he made from selling the wool helped build hospitals for soldiers wounded in the war.

President Harry Truman loved to play the piano and had three pianos in the White House. One of them broke through the second floor. Shortly after that, Congress voted to rebuild the White House, which was falling apart.

Lyndon Johnson loved to talk so much that he had phones everywhere. Some phones were marked POTUS (President of the United States). Johnson had phones in bathrooms, cars, boats, and planes. He even had a special floating phone on a raft in the White House swimming pool.

THE FIRST LADIES

Martha Washington, George Washington's wife, was called Lady Washington. This led to the name First Lady, which is now used for all Presidents' wives.

James Madison was President in 1812, when the United States was at war with Great Britain. When the British burned the White House, Madison's wife, Dolley, refused to leave behind a painting of George Washington. Mrs. Madison ordered her servants to break the glass and cut the picture from the frame. The painting now hangs in the East Room of the White House.

When Woodrow Wilson became ill, his wife, Edith, became his advisor. Many people called her the "Secret President" because they felt that she was running the country.

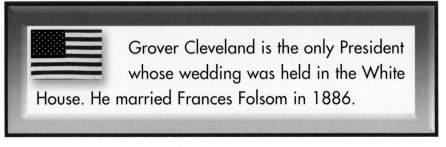

Grover Cleveland is the only President whose wedding was held in the White House. He married Frances Folsom in 1886.

Eleanor Roosevelt

Hilary Rodham Clinton

Eleanor Roosevelt, wife of President Franklin Roosevelt, wanted to be "plain, ordinary Mrs. Roosevelt." However, she became a very important First Lady. She was the first First Lady to speak out on important issues. She fought for the rights of working women, African Americans, and **immigrants**. In later years she was called "First Lady of the World."

Hilary Rodham Clinton was the first First Lady to win an election. In 2000 she became a senator for the state of New York.

THE PRESIDENTS' CHILDREN

In 1800 Susanna Adams was the first child to live in the White House. She was the granddaughter of President John Adams and his wife, Abigail. Since then many children have filled the White House with their energy and laughter.

Nellie Grant, Ulysses S. Grant's daughter, was born on the Fourth of July. When she was little, she thought that people set off fireworks to celebrate her birthday.

President Grover Cleveland's first child, a daughter, was nicknamed Baby Ruth. A well-known candy bar was named for her. Esther, his second daughter, is the only President's child born in the White House.

President Theodore Roosevelt called his children his "blessed bunnies" and stopped working at four o'clock every day to play with them. "I play bear with the children almost every night," he said. The Roosevelt children were allowed to run wild through the White House. They roller-skated through the East Room, played hide and seek in the attic, and slid down the stairs on serving trays. The boys were so wild that newspapers nicknamed them "the White House Gang."

John Tyler had more children than any other President. He was the father of 15 children.

President and Mrs. George W. Bush brought two dogs (Spot and Barney) and a cat named India to the White House. Their other cat, Ernie, was too wild for the White House. He went to live with a family in California.

WHITE HOUSE PETS

The explorers Lewis and Clarke brought grizzly bears to Thomas Jefferson. Jefferson kept them on the White House lawn, where everyone could see them. Jefferson also had a pet mockingbird that rode on his shoulder and took food from his mouth!

Tad, Robert, and Willie, the three sons of Abraham Lincoln, had all the pets they wanted. Tad Lincoln rode through the East Room on a chair pulled by two goats. The boys even had a pet turkey named Jack, who had been saved from becoming Thanksgiving dinner.

When Archibald Roosevelt, Theodore Roosevelt's son, was sick with measles, his brothers brought his pony into the White House to visit him. The pony and the children squeezed into the White House elevator and rode to the second floor! Theodore Roosevelt also kept many other animals at the White House, including five bears, two parrots, a lion, a zebra, a barn owl, snakes, lizards, rats, roosters, and a raccoon.

President Warren G. Harding loved his Airedale terrier, Laddie Boy. When Harding hit golf balls on the White House lawn, Laddie Boy retrieved them.

The most famous Presidential pet of all time is Fala, Franklin Roosevelt's Scottish terrier. Fala went almost everywhere with Roosevelt. A statue of Fala sits next to a statue of Roosevelt at the F.D.R. Memorial in Washington, D.C.

John F. Kennedy's children, Carolyn and John, kept many pets at the White House. They had rabbits, hamsters, parakeets, guinea pigs, and a pony named Macaroni. They also had a dog named Pushinka. She was the daughter of the first Russian space dog to orbit the earth.

President Franklin Roosevelt with Fala

31

President Lyndon Johnson singing with Yuki

President Lyndon Johnson had several dogs, including two beagles, which he named Him and Her. One of Johnson's favorite dogs was his beloved mutt Yuki. Johnson's daughter Luci found Yuki at a Texas gas station.

When William Clinton was President, Socks, the First Cat, and Buddy, the First Dog, were almost as popular as the President. They received more than 300,000 letters, pictures, and e-mail messages from fans in almost 50 countries, as well as hundreds of gifts. Volunteers helped Socks and Buddy reply to all the mail.

CHAPTER 6
ELECTING THE PRESIDENT

Many people would like to be President, but not everyone can. The Constitution has rules about who can be President. The person must be at least 35 years old. He or she must have been born in the United States. In addition, he or she must have lived in the United States for 14 years or longer.

Even if a person meets those rules and others, he or she must first be **nominated,** or chosen, by a **political party**. The Republicans and Democrats are the two main political parties in the United States. The person nominated by a party is called a **candidate**.

Every four years, each party picks a candidate to run for President. The candidates **campaign** across the country to get people to vote for them. They give speeches telling why they should be President. They pass out posters and buttons.

Election Day is the first Tuesday in November. On that day people vote for the person they think will make the best President. Before the election of 1920, most women were not allowed to vote. African Americans were not allowed to vote until 1964, when the Civil Rights Act was passed.

George Bush campaigning for President

The January 20th that follows the election is called Inauguration Day. On that day the new President takes office. In a ceremony in Washington, D.C., the President raises his right hand. Then he repeats the oath of office:

I do solemnly swear that I will faithfully execute the Office of President of the United States and will, to the best of my ability, preserve, protect, and defend the Constitution of the United States.

When the new President takes the oath of office, he is promising to do his best job as leader of the country.

The President serves the United States for four years. This is called his term of office. Then there is another election. The President

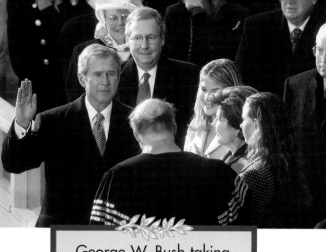

George W. Bush taking the oath of office

can be elected again for a second term.

The President is powerful, but the voters have even more power. If they do not like a President, they do not have to elect that person for a second term. "The President *is* Commander-in-Chief," Franklin Roosevelt told future Presidents, "[but] he, too, has his superior officers—the people of the United States."

President Franklin Roosevelt was the only President to serve three terms (1933–1937, 1937–1941, 1941–1945). After that, Congress changed the Constitution. Now a President can serve only two terms.

THE U.S. PRESIDENTS

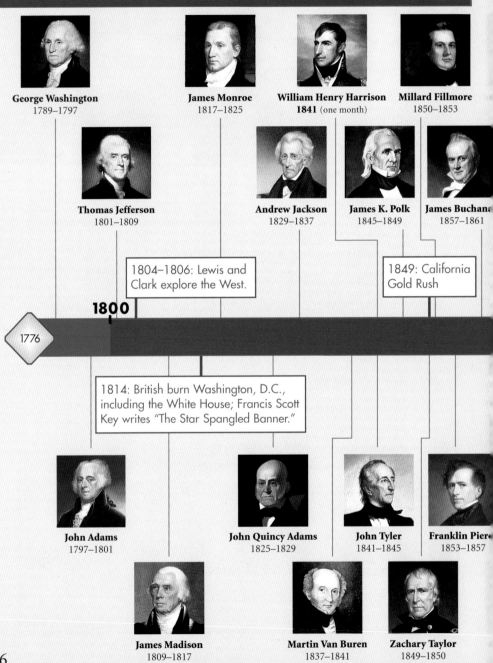

George Washington
1789–1797

James Monroe
1817–1825

William Henry Harrison
1841 (one month)

Millard Fillmore
1850–1853

Thomas Jefferson
1801–1809

Andrew Jackson
1829–1837

James K. Polk
1845–1849

James Buchana
1857–1861

1804–1806: Lewis and Clark explore the West.

1849: California Gold Rush

1800

1776

1814: British burn Washington, D.C., including the White House; Francis Scott Key writes "The Star Spangled Banner."

John Adams
1797–1801

John Quincy Adams
1825–1829

John Tyler
1841–1845

Franklin Pier
1853–1857

James Madison
1809–1817

Martin Van Buren
1837–1841

Zachary Taylor
1849–1850

foreign (FAWR uhn) relating to another country

government (GUHV uhr muhnt) a system of controlling a city, state, or country and managing its affairs

immigrants (IHM uh gruhnts) people who come from another country to live in a new country

military (MIHL uh tehr ee) the armed forces of a country

nation (NAY shuhn) a country

nominated (NAHM uh nayt id) chosen to run for office

official (uh FISH uhl) having been decided by a person who holds an office or is in charge

political party (puh LIT uh kuhl PAHR tee) a group of people with similar beliefs who try to shape and direct the actions of the government

press conference (pres KAHN fuhr uhns) a meeting with people who report the news for newspapers, radio, and television

terms (tuhrmz) certain periods of time

treaties (TREE teez) formal agreements made between two or more groups or countries

INDEX

Air Force One 21–22

Blue Room 17

Cabinet 7, 10, 17, 20

Cabinet Room 17

Camp David 23

Chief Executive 9–10

Civil Rights Act 34

Clinton, Hilary
    Rodham 28

Commander-in-Chief 10

Congress 12, 21

East Room 17, 27

Easter Egg Roll 23–24

Election Day 34

Executive Branch
    5, 9–10, 20

Federal system 4–5

Foreign affairs 12

Great Britain 4, 27

Hamilton, Alexander 7

Head of State 11, 21

Inauguration Day 34

Madison, Dolley 27

Marine One 23

Oath of office 6, 34

Oval Office 21

Revolutionary War 4

Roosevelt, Eleanor 28

State Dining Room 17

State of the Union
    Address 13

United States
    Constitution 4–6, 33

Vice-President 17

War of 1812 15, 27

Washington, D.C. 8, 31

West Wing 15, 17, 20

Wilson, Edith 27

World War I 12, 26